Also available in the series...

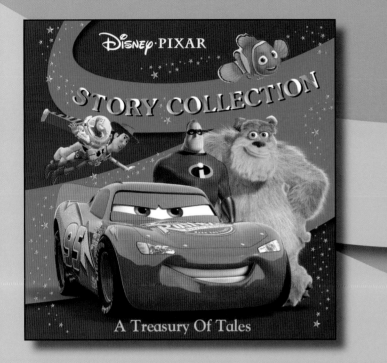

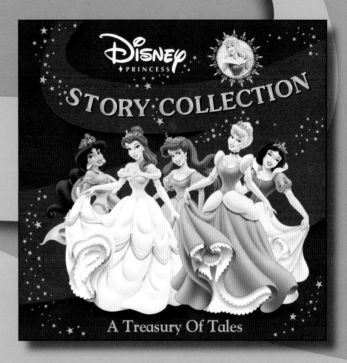

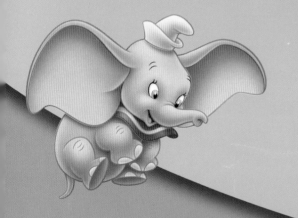

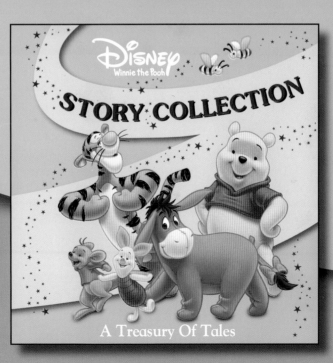

Disney

STORY
COLLECTION

Bath · New York · Singapore · Hong Kong · Cologne · Delhi · Melbourne

TABLE OF CONTENTS

First published by Parragon in 2007

Parragon
Queen Street House
4 Queen Street
Bath BA1 1HE, UK

ISBN 978-1-4054-9833-3
Printed in China

Friends Forever

On a distant planet, a blue creature named Experiment 626 stood before the Grand Council. His creator, Jumba Jukiba, was with him. Experiment 626 destroyed everything he touched and Jumba had been accused of creating a monster.

The Grand Councilwoman turned to 626. "Show us there is something inside you that is good," she said.

"*Meega, na la queesta!*" replied 626.

"So naughty!" the Grand Councilwoman gasped. "It has no place among us. Take it away!"

Experiment 626 was put on a spaceship that would drop him off on a distant planet. However, before he could reach his new home, 626 escaped in a police cruiser. He headed straight for Earth and the tiny island of Kauai.

The Grand Councilwoman sent Jumba and an Earth expert named Pleakley to retrieve 626.

Meanwhile, on the island of Kauai, there was a little girl named Lilo. Lilo was running as quickly as she could, as she was late for her hula class.

When she arrived, Lilo scurried into line, leaving a trail of saltwater behind her. The other dancers slipped on the wet floor and toppled over.

"Stop!" yelled her teacher. "Lilo, why are you all wet?"

She explained how she had dived into the water to feed a fish a peanut butter sandwich.

"You're crazy," said Mertle, one of the dancers.

Lilo pounced on her.

"Lilo!" yelled her teacher, pulling her away.

"I'm sorry," said Lilo. "I'll be good."

However, none of the other dancers wanted Lilo to stay, so she had to go home. Lilo was very lonely. She didn't have any friends; her parents were gone and her big sister, Nani, though a good big sister, was having a hard time learning how to be a parent. To top it all off, a social worker was threatening to take Lilo away from Nani.

That night, the sisters got in a huge fight. Lilo went to her room and slammed the door shut. Nani went upstairs and apologized.

Suddenly, Lilo saw something flash in the night sky. "A falling star!" she cried. "Get out, I have to make a wish."

Nani went into the hallway but stayed by the door so she could hear her sister's wish.

"I need someone to be my friend," Lilo whispered.

Nani hadn't realized how lonely her little sister was. Tomorrow, she decided, they would get a dog to keep Lilo company.

The flash Lilo had seen was Experiment 626's ship crashing on the island. A truck driver found him and took him to an animal shelter. All the other animals were scared of 626, but he didn't care. He scrunched two of his four arms in towards his torso so he would look more like a dog. That way, he'd be adopted and have a place to hide from the aliens who were chasing him.

Lilo and Nani soon arrived at the shelter.

"Hi!" Lilo said when she saw 626.

"Hi," the creature replied and then gave her a hug.

Lilo walked back to the front room and told Nani she'd found the dog she wanted. "He's good," she said. "I can tell. His name is . . . Stitch."

They took Stitch home even though Nani thought he looked strange.

Nani was glad Lilo finally had a friend. When Nani left for work, Lilo and Stitch went for a ride, on Lilo's bicycle. They rode all around the island, even stopping for ice cream along the way. Stitch was wild, but he and Lilo had fun.

Later, at the restaurant where Nani worked, Stitch spotted Jumba and Pleakley, who were dressed as tourists. When the aliens tried to capture Stitch, he almost bit Pleakley's head off.

Nani's manager was furious and fired her. It was just the kind of thing Lilo and Nani didn't need.

At home, Stitch also began to tear things apart.

"We have to take him back," Nani said.

"We adopted him!" Lilo cried. "What about 'ohana'? Dad said 'ohana means family! Family means—"

"Nobody gets left behind," Nani finished. "I know." She remembered how welcoming her parents had been and how important family was to them. She changed her mind. She would give Stitch another chance - for Lilo's sake.

That night, while Lilo was sleeping, Stitch found a book called *The Ugly Duckling.* He looked through it and noticed that the duckling was by himself a lot, just like him.

He woke up Lilo and showed her the book. She explained that the duckling was sad because he didn't fit in. Stitch knew how that felt. He wanted to feel like he belonged somewhere, too.

Lilo decided to show Stitch how to be good so that he would fit in. First, she tried to teach him hula dancing. He did pretty well until his twirls got a little out of control.

Then, they tried the ukulele. At first, Stitch was rather good. All of a sudden, he began to play the instrument like a heavy metal guitar and *smash!* All of the windows around him shattered.

Finally, Lilo took him to the beach. Here, she decided, he could show everyone what he had learned and how good he could be. Stitch grabbed his ukulele and waddled to the shoreline in front of all the tourists. He began twanging away.

The tourists loved the music and swarmed around him, taking pictures. The flashes were too bright for Stitch though, he grabbed a camera and smashed it to bits. A man soaked him with a squirt gun. The blasts of water made Stitch angrier. He grabbed the tourist and hurled him through the air. Everyone ran away as fast as they could. They were frightened.

Lilo was upset. Stitch hadn't learned to be good. Plus, the social worker saw what had happened and was worried about Lilo's safety.

That night, Lilo decided to talk to Stitch. "Our family's little, now," she told him. "But if you want, you could be part of it."

Stitch knew that he had made life harder for Lilo and Nani. He turned towards the window.

" '*Ohana* means family," Lilo continued. "Family means nobody gets left behind. But if you want to leave, you can."

Stitch climbed out the window and headed into the night.

When Lilo woke up, she told her sister that Stitch had left. "It's good he's gone," she said, trying not to sound upset. "We don't need him."

"Lilo," Nani consoled her, "sometimes you try your hardest, but things don't work out the way you want them to. Sometimes things have to change . . . and maybe sometimes they're for the best." She then left Lilo and went to another job.

Meanwhile, Jumba had found Stitch and was chasing him through the forest. Stitch realized he didn't want to leave, after all, Lilo was his friend. He ran back to the house.

When Lilo saw him, she knew she had to help. "What are we going to do?" she asked.

Together, they fought Jumba, but it was a losing battle. In the process, the aliens destroyed Lilo and Nani's house. Lilo ran into the forest, she was devastated. Stitch followed her.

"You ruined everything!" she told him.

At that moment, Captain Gantu, another alien sent to capture 626, trapped them and put them in a containment pod on his ship. Stitch escaped, but the ship took off, with Lilo inside!

Stitch knew he had to save Lilo. She was the only friend he had in the entire galaxy. Stitch found Nani and was able to convince Jumba and Pleakley to help them rescue Lilo. They fired up the police cruiser and raced after her.

They got close to Gantu's ship and Stitch jumped out of the cruiser. He landed on the windshield and crawled towards Lilo, but Gantu managed to shake him off.

Lilo saw her friend. "Don't leave me, okay?" she cried.

"Okay," he replied.

Stitch managed to get back to Gantu's ship. He climbed through the windshield, threw Gantu off, and rescued Lilo.

"You came back," she said.

"Nobody gets left behind," he replied. He finally understood how important family was.

With Lilo in his arms, Stitch leaped onto the cruiser as Nani, Jumba and Pleakley flew by.

They went to the beach where the Grand Councilwoman was waiting to take Stitch home. "This is my family," Stitch said, pointing to Lilo and Nani. He was allowed to stay on Earth and the social worker decided not to take Lilo away from her sister. Lilo and Stitch hugged each other happily. They knew they would be friends forever.

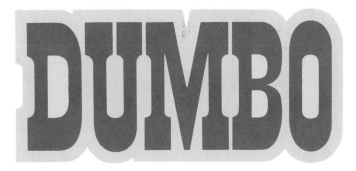

Dumbo Takes Flight

"Isn't he cute!" the lady elephants cooed when the baby elephant was delivered to the circus train. "Isn't he a darling?" Mrs Jumbo beamed with pride at her new son, Jumbo Junior.

"*Ah . . . ahh . . . choo!*" The baby elephant sneezed. His whole body shook and his ears suddenly uncurled. They were huge - much bigger than a normal elephant's ears. The lady elephants gasped and shook their heads in disapproval. "Just look at those ears!" they said.

"Precious little Jumbo," one lady elephant said mockingly.

"Jumbo? You mean Dumbo!" another cried. They all laughed. From that day on, everyone called the little elephant *Dumbo*. Mrs Jumbo ignored them. As far as she was concerned, her son was perfect.

Soon, the train arrived in town. Once the equipment was unloaded and the tents were pitched, the circus parade began! A band played merrily and the crowd cheered as the animals marched through the streets. Dumbo followed his mother, but his ears were so big that he tripped over them and fell into a mud puddle!

A bunch of children jeered at the little elephant and began to taunt him. They pulled his ears so hard that Dumbo fell over when they let go!

Mrs Jumbo was furious. She picked up a bale of hay and threw it to the ground. The people who ran the circus were worried she might hurt someone, so they put chains around her and locked her in a circus wagon - by herself.

Heartbroken, Dumbo sat in a corner and cried. The other elephants sniggered. It was all his fault, they decided. "Yes, him with those ears that only a mother could love," one of them said.

When Dumbo walked by, the other elephants pretended not to see him. Nobody wanted to talk to him. The baby elephant was all alone.

Luckily, Timothy Q. Mouse was sitting nearby. "Poor little guy!" he said to himself. "There he goes, without a friend in the world." The mouse decided to help. He sneaked up to the elephants. "You like to pick on little guys, huh?" he shouted.

"Well, why don't you pick on me!" The elephants ran away quickly, as they were all scared of mice.

Dumbo was afraid of the mouse, too. He hid in a haystack. Timothy tried to coax him out. "Look, Dumbo," the mouse said, "I'm your friend! Come on out!" But the little elephant just shook his head.

Timothy finally got Dumbo to come out by offering him a peanut and some promises. He told Dumbo he'd help him find his mother again. First, though, he was going to come up with a circus act for the little elephant.

The ringmaster decided to try something new the next night: a pyramid of elephants. Timothy convinced him to make Dumbo the grand finale. The young elephant was supposed to jump on a springboard and catapult to the top of the pyramid.

When Dumbo tried it, though, he smashed into the bottom of the pyramid, causing the rest of the elephants to tumble to the ground and the circus tent to collapse.

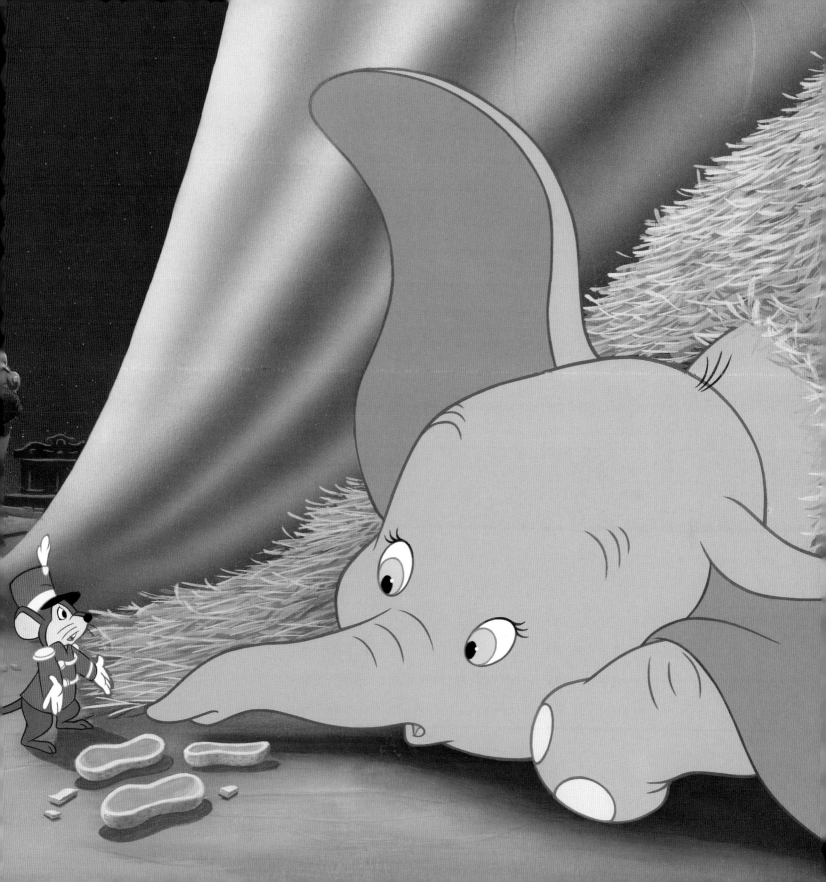

The elephants were bruised, bandaged and embarrassed. They couldn't wait to get back at Dumbo. The ringmaster was angry at him too and he decided to make the little elephant into a clown.

The other clowns painted Dumbo's face and dressed him like a baby. They even made him wear a nappy. As flames leaped up all around him, the clowns pretended to rescue him from a burning building. They even threw water in his face! As if that wasn't bad enough, the clowns then pushed him off a tall tower and into a tub of plaster. The audience loved the act, but Dumbo felt ashamed.

After the show, Timothy tried to cheer up the elephant. "You're a big hit!" he announced. "You ought to be proud!"

Dumbo just looked at the ground. If this was what being a star was like, he didn't want any part of it.

Timothy stood on a cake of soap and helped the elephant clean the makeup off of his face. "Come on!" he nudged his friend. "I gotta wash behind your ears!" Dumbo barely managed to smile.

Before long, big tears trickled down Dumbo's face. Timothy didn't know how to make his friend feel better. Then he thought of something. He snapped his fingers. "I forgot to tell ya. We're going over to see your mother!"

The mouse led Dumbo to the wagon where Mrs Jumbo tied up. The baby elephant stood on his hind legs and peered in anxiously at his mother. Mrs Jumbo tried to come to the window, but the chains held her back. Luckily, her trunk fit between the bars. She scooped her baby up and rocked him, soothing him with a lullaby. Dumbo felt safe and peaceful.

When it was time to say good-bye, mother and son held on to each other for as long as they could.

As he and Timothy returned to the tent, Dumbo began to cry. The mouse tried to comfort him. "We may have had a lot of hard luck up till now," Timothy said, "but you and me are gonna do big things together." Dumbo was still sad, but it was nice to have a friend who believed in him.

The next day, Timothy woke up and noticed that he and Dumbo were in a tree. He had no idea how they had got there. While the elephant slept, the mouse tried to figure it out. "Now, let's see," he mused. "Elephants can't climb trees, can they? Naw. . . that's ridiculous! Couldn't jump up! Uh-uh, it's too high!"

A group of crows were sitting on a branch above them. "Hey there, son - maybe you all flew up!" the crow said. Timothy laughed, then stopped. "That's it!" he cried. Suddenly everything made sense! Timothy grabbed one of Dumbo's ears and shouted, "Why didn't I think of this before? Your ears . . . they're perfect wings! The very things that held you down are going to carry you up!"

It took a while to convince Dumbo, though. Timothy had a thought, he handed him a feather and told him it had magical powers that would make him fly, Dumbo spread his ears and soared through the air!

Under the big top that night, Dumbo stood on the top of the burning tower, clutching his magic feather. He was about to surprise the whole circus with his flying. Dumbo jumped and the feather slipped from his grasp! He plummeted toward the ground, paralyzed with fear. Timothy urged him on, shouting, "The magic feather was just a gag! You can fly! Honest you can!"

Right before he hit the floor, Dumbo spread his ears. Maybe Timothy was right. Then the most amazing thing happened, he began to fly. He flew higher and higher, even doing loop-the-loops. The audience were amazed.

The next day, Dumbo made headlines in the newspapers. Soon, he was setting world records and appearing in films, too! Just as Timothy had predicted, Dumbo was a star!

None of the other animals dared to make fun of him now - Dumbo was the circus's main attraction. He had his own car on the circus train, even though he usually flew. But when Dumbo needed a rest, he would stop to see his mother, who'd finally been freed. And he always kept a special place in his heart for his faithful friend, Timothy Q. Mouse.

Disney's POCAHONTAS

Friends in a New Land

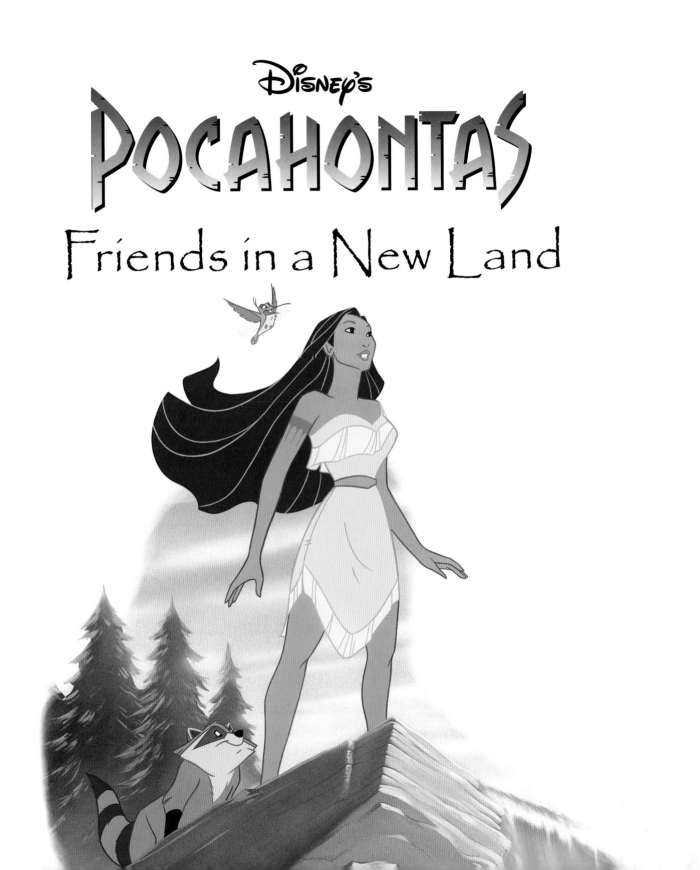

High on a cliff, an Indian princess named Pocahontas was exploring the forest with her friends Meeko; a raccoon and Flit; a hummingbird. Although the two creatures didn't always get along, both loved Pocahontas and were almost always with her.

Suddenly, Pocahontas's friend Nakoma called to her from the river. "Your father's back!" she shouted. "Come down here." Pocahontas began to run through the forest, then turned and jumped off of the cliff instead. She swan-dived into the crystal blue river and swam over to Nakoma's canoe.

Meeko leaped off of the cliff after Pocahontas. He grabbed Flit nervously on the way down and they dropped into the river with a splash.

Breathlessly, Meeko scrambled into the canoe, shook himself off and took his usual lookout post at the front. Flit, annoyed at the raccoon for getting him wet, hovered in the air as Pocahontas and Nakoma steered the canoe home.

When they arrived back at the village, Chief Powhatan was happy to see Pocahontas. "Kocoum has asked to seek your hand in marriage," he told his daughter. "He will make a good husband."

"But he's so serious," Pocahontas replied unhappily.

Meeko agreed. When Powhatan wasn't looking, the raccoon puffed up his chest and made a grim face, pretending to be Kocoum. The silly animal could always make Pocahontas laugh.

Still, the young woman was troubled. She went to see the ancient tree spirit, Grandmother Willow, to ask for her advice. Pocahontas told her about a spinning arrow she kept seeing in a dream.

"It is pointing you down your path," the wise spirit told her.

As Pocahontas tried to figure out what her path was, she climbed high into the branches of Grandmother Willow, with Meeko and Flit close behind. They saw something they'd never seen before: a large boat with sails that Pocahontas mistook for clouds. It was the *Susan Constant*, a ship filled with English settlers seeking gold.

A while later, Pocahontas saw one of the settlers exploring the forest. She was curious but cautious as she hid behind some bushes. However, Meeko was a very mischievous raccoon. He always thought with his stomach . . . and followed his nose. He scurried toward the man and poked his nose into the settler's bag.

"Well, you're a strange-looking fellow," said the man, who was named John Smith. "You hungry?"

He handed the raccoon a biscuit. Meeko nibbled happily.

Still hidden, Pocahontas smiled. She was glad to see this stranger being so generous to her friend.

Flit, on the other hand, was worried about Pocahontas. Even if Meeko had got them into this mess, the hummingbird would do his best to get them out of it. Ever protective, he flew straight at the newcomer, poking at him and trying to make him leave. Luckily, Smith got called away by one of the other settlers.

Soon, Pocahontas met John Smith face to face. As they got to know each other, she showed him how the land and water, the people and animals, were all connected to one another. John Smith was fascinated with all that Pocahontas had to teach.

Meeko was fascinated, too - with Smith's bag! The raccoon eagerly searched for more biscuits. But Flit, on the other hand, circled angrily around Smith's head.

"Flit just doesn't like strangers," Pocahontas explained to John Smith.

"Well, I'm not a stranger anymore," Smith said. He extended a finger to Flit, but the bird just poked it with his sharp beak.

"Stubborn little fellow, isn't he?" Smith said.

"Very stubborn," Pocahontas agreed.

Just then, Meeko popped out of Smith's bag. In his paw was a compass. It was too hard to eat, but Meeko hid his discovery in Grandmother Willow's branches anyway.

Meanwhile, at the settler's camp, Percy, a very spoiled dog, sat on a pillow, feeling lazy and looking smug. He was the pet pug of Governor Ratcliffe, who had been on the ship that brought the settlers to this new land. Percy had always had an easy life. His pillows were the finest and the fluffiest. And he was always given the most delicious food. He was one pampered pooch . . . until Meeko showed up!

The always-hungry raccoon had followed John Smith to his camp. It wasn't long before Meeko spied Percy's fine dinner. With a quick hand, he shoved it all into his mouth.

Percy was furious when he saw what the raccoon had done! Barking wildly, the dog ran after Meeko.

Percy chased him out of the camp and into the forest, near Grandmother Willow. Pocahontas and John Smith were there, too.

Smith had hurried back after learning that the settlers wanted to attack the Indians and he and Pocahontas were trying to figure out how to keep the peace. They had realized how much the settlers and the Indians could teach each other.

Percy growled at Meeko and continued to chase him.

"Meeko!" scolded Pocahontas.

John Smith shook his head. "You see what I mean? Once two sides want to fight, nothing can stop them."

Nothing except Grandmother Willow. "All right, that's enough!" the ancient tree spirit said to the animals.

Percy was so stunned to see a talking tree that he fainted!

A bit later, Grandmother Willow dipped one of her branches into the river. It caused the water to ripple outwards. She explained that although the ripples were very small at first, they quickly grew larger. "But someone has to start them," she said.

Pocahontas and John Smith knew that the tree spirit was trying to get them to change the way the Indians and the settlers felt about each other. They agreed to talk to Chief Powhatan to see if peace could be reached.

They never made it, though. Along the way, an Indian warrior attacked Smith. Then, another settler shot the warrior, but Smith took the blame. He was taken prisoner and led to the Indian village.

Flit, Meeko and Percy watched the whole thing from the base of a tree. As Flit and Meeko began to follow Pocahontas back to the village, they turned and saw poor Percy, shaking with fear. Then the most surprising thing happened: Meeko laid a comforting paw on Percy's head and the pug stopped shaking. With a nod, Meeko let Percy know he could come with them.

Back at the village, the new friends looked on with sadness as Pocahontas visited John Smith. The Indians had decided he would die the next morning.

"I'm so sorry!" she cried. "It would have been better if we'd never met. None of this would have happened."

"Pocahontas, I'd rather die tomorrow than live a hundred years without knowing you," John Smith told her.

Pocahontas was heartbroken. She went back to see Grandmother Willow. "What can I do?" she asked sadly.

Meeko wanted to help his friend. Trying to cheer up Pocahontas, he handed her John Smith's compass, which he had hidden.

Looking at it, Pocahontas saw the spinning arrow that she had dreamed about.

Now she knew what path to follow. Quickly, she ran to the village and stepped in front of John Smith, willing to give up her life to protect him.

Chief Powhatan laid down his weapon, but the settlers had arrived. Governor Ratcliffe fired his gun.

"No!" yelled Smith. He jumped in front of the Indian chief, taking the bullet himself.

John Smith knew he would have to return to London to have his wounds treated. He and Pocahontas said good-bye, and he was carried to the ship. Everyone was sad to see him go.

Percy decided to stay in the new land with Meeko and Flit and they were happy to have him around. They watched as John Smith sailed away, thinking about how much had happened and what a wonderful surprise their new friendships had turned out to be.

THE JUNGLE BOOK

Mowgli Finds a Friend

One day, deep in the jungles of India, a strange sound echoed through the trees. Bagheera the panther heard the noise and ran along the riverbank. He followed it until he found a boat that had landed on the shore. Inside, a baby boy was crying. When the baby saw the panther, he smiled. Bagheera decided to take the boy to a wolf family that lived nearby. The mother had just had a litter of pups and Bagheera thought she might be able to look after one more baby.

When the mother wolf saw the boy, she agreed to take care of him. She named him Mowgli and for ten years she raised him as one of her own. Mowgli was a very happy Man-cub. He spent his days running and playing with his wolf brothers and sisters.

One day, bad news arrived in the jungle. Shere Khan the tiger had returned after a long absence. The tiger was mean and hated everything. More than anything though, Shere Khan hated Man.

This meant that it was no longer safe for Mowgli to live in the jungle. The wolves decided that he should go to a Man-village at once.

Bagheera had kept watch over Mowgli through the years and volunteered to take him. The wolves accepted his offer. Later that night, the boy rode on the panther's back as they made their way through the jungle. Mowgli soon grew tired.

"Shouldn't we start back home?" he asked sleepily.

Bagheera shook his head. "We're not going back," the panther said. "I'm taking you to the Man-village."

But Mowgli did not want to leave the jungle. It was his home. "I don't want to go to the Man-village!" he shouted. Then he added, "I can take care of myself."

"You wouldn't last one day," Bagheera said. Then he led Mowgli up a tree where they would sleep for the night.

The next morning, Bagheera was ready to continue to the village. Mowgli grabbed on to a nearby tree trunk. "I'm staying right here," he declared. The panther tried to pull him away, but Mowgli held on tight. Finally, Bagheera pulled so hard that he lost his grip and went flying into a large pond.

"That does it!" cried the panther. "From now on, you're on your own." Then Bagheera walked off into the jungle and disappeared.

Mowgli headed in the opposite direction. "I can take care of myself," he said aloud. Some time later, he sat down in the shade. As he rested, he began to worry that maybe he *couldn't* take care of himself.

Just then, a bear named Baloo walked out of the jungle and spotted him. A Man-cub in the jungle was an unusual sight, so the friendly bear walked over to sniff him. Mowgli reached out and slapped Baloo right on the nose.

"Ouch!" the bear cried. "I'm just trying to be friendly!"

"Go away and leave me alone," Mowgli said with a scowl.

But Baloo did not listen. He sat down next to the Man-cub and patted him on the back. "That's pretty big talk, Little Britches," the bear said. He then decided that Mowgli needed to have some fun. Baloo jumped up and started bobbing and weaving like a boxer. "Hey, kid, Baloo's gonna learn you to fight like a bear."

The bear's silly behaviour made Mowgli laugh and soon he was dancing around and boxing just like Baloo. When they finished, Mowgli jumped up on his new friend's stomach and tickled him. "You're all right, kid," Baloo said gently.

Just then, Bagheera walked over to them. He had returned to make sure Mowgli was okay. The panther told Baloo that he thought Mowgli should go to the Man-village so he'd be safe from Shere Khan.

Baloo didn't want his little buddy to go to a Man-village. "They'll ruin him. They'll make a man out of him," the bear said.

Bagheera sighed. He knew Mowgli would never leave now that he had made friends with Baloo. The panther watched as the pair jumped into the river and floated lazily away.

Suddenly, a group of monkeys grabbed Mowgli! They began to toss him back and forth. "Give me back my Man-cub!" shouted Baloo. The monkeys ignored the bear and carried Mowgli away. Baloo found Bagheera and the two followed the monkeys deep into the jungle.

The monkeys took Mowgli to their leader, King Louie, who lived amid ancient ruins. The monkey king wanted to make a deal. If the Man-cub taught him how to make fire, then Louie would help him stay in the jungle.

"But I don't know how to make fire," said Mowgli.

King Louie didn't believe him. He danced around, trying to convince the Man-cub to tell him the secret of Man's fire.

When Bagheera and Baloo arrived at the ruins, they saw Mowgli dancing with the monkeys. Bagheera told Baloo to distract the king. The bear knew exactly what to do. He dressed up like a big female monkey and batted his eyelashes at King Louie.

Just as Bagheera was about to rescue Mowgli, Baloo's disguise fell off. The monkeys chased the three friends all over the ruins. Then Louie ran into a column and the ruins began to fall down. Mowgli, Baloo and Bagheera hurried away.

Later, as Mowgli lay sleeping, Bagheera tried to make Baloo see that the Man-cub wasn't safe in the jungle - especially with Shere Khan around. Baloo knew the panther was right.

The next morning, Baloo and the Man-cub began walking.

"Where are we going?" Mowgli asked after a while.

Baloo gulped. "Ah, look, little buddy . . . I need to take you to the Man-village. It's where you belong," he stammered.

"But you said we were partners!" Mowgli yelled. "You said I could stay with you!" The Man-cub raced away. Sadly, he sat down on a log as a light rain began to fall. All of a sudden, Shere Khan appeared! "You don't scare me," Mowgli said. He picked up a heavy branch and prepared to fight the tiger.

Shere Khan snarled and lunged at Mowgli.
Just as Shere Khan was about to land on the Man-cub, he crashed to the ground. Baloo had arrived and grabbed on to the tiger's tail! "Run, Mowgli, run!" the bear cried.

While Baloo struggled to keep the tiger away from Mowgli, lightning struck nearby, causing a fire. The Man-cub picked up a burning branch and tied it to Shere Khan's tail.

When the mighty tiger saw the fire, he let out a terrified roar and ran for his life.

Mowgli had defeated Shere Khan! But not everyone had escaped unharmed. Baloo was lying on the ground . . . and he wasn't moving.

"Baloo, get up," Mowgli begged. But Baloo didn't respond.

Bagheera walked into the clearing. Seeing the bear lying on the ground, he started to comfort Mowgli.

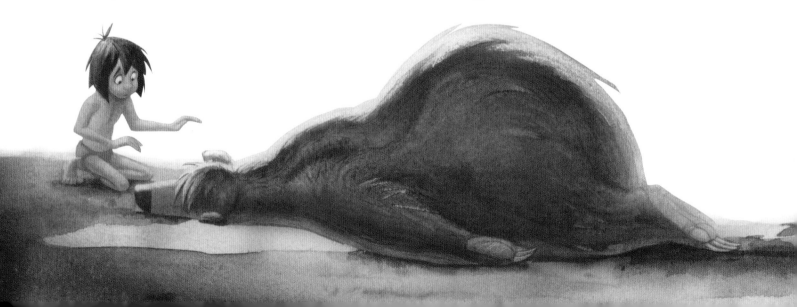

Suddenly, the panther was interrupted by a familiar voice. "I'm all right, Little Britches!" cried Baloo. "I was just taking five, you know, playing it cool."

"Baloo, you're alive!" Mowgli exclaimed, throwing his arms around his friend.

After Baloo got up, the three friends left the clearing and made their way back into the jungle. Suddenly, Mowgli heard someone singing. "I want to take a closer look," he told Baloo and Bagheera. Climbing up a tree, he saw a girl. When she noticed him, she giggled. Mowgli turned to his friends and shrugged his shoulders.

Baloo and Bagheera watched as he began to follow her into the Man-village. "Mowgli, come back!" Baloo cried.

"Let him go," said Bagheera.

Baloo sighed. He knew it was the right thing to do. His little friend had a new home. "I still think he would have made a great bear," Baloo said. Then, he put his arm around Bagheera and the two headed back into the jungle, happy that their friend was going to the place where he belonged.

Disney's

THE LION KING

A Lion's Best Friends

Mufasa, the lion king, was the ruler of the Pride Lands. When his son, Simba, was born, the animals bowed in respect as the wise baboon, Rafiki, presented the cub. They knew that someday Simba would be their leader. It was all part of the Circle of Life.

Until Simba was born, his uncle Scar had been next in line to be king. There was nothing that the greedy lion wanted more. So he devised an evil plan.

"Your father has a surprise for you," Scar told his nephew one morning as he led him into a deep gorge. "Just stay on this rock and I'll go get him."

Eager for his surprise, the cub obeyed. He didn't know that Scar had instructed some hyenas to scare a herd of wildebeests into a stampede, straight towards him! Nor did the cub know that Scar had run off to warn Mufasa that his only son was in danger.

It was a trap; and it worked!

Just as Scar had hoped, Mufasa leaped into the gorge and raced towards Simba, who was dangling from a branch. By the time the lion king carried Simba to the safety of a rocky ledge, he had become very tired.

For a moment, the stampeding wildebeests almost carried Mufasa away. But he clung to the rocky gorge wall and slowly began to claw his way up the side.

"Brother, help me!" Mufasa cried to Scar.

Instead of helping, though, Scar dug his claws into his brother's paws. He smiled wickedly as Mufasa fell to his death.

Unfortunately for Scar, Simba was still alive. But the evil lion knew just how to get rid of him.

"If it weren't for you, your father would still be alive," he told the cub, who hadn't seen what Scar had done. "Run away . . . and never return!"

So that is just what Simba did.

Simba ran until the ground grew hard and cracked beneath his blistered paws and his small, sore legs collapsed from exhaustion.

He fell asleep at once. When Simba woke up, things were very different.

The desert had turned into a lush jungle. Instead of being

alone, he was with a warthog named Pumbaa and a meerkat named Timon.

"We saved you!" cried the meerkat.

Timon and Pumbaa could tell that something was bothering Simba. However, the lion cub didn't want to talk about it and that was just fine with them.

Their motto, after all, was *hakuna matata*, which meant *no worries!*

"You got to put your past behind you," Timon told Simba. Timon and Pumbaa didn't care about what the cub thought he had done.

They liked him and wanted him to stay in the jungle. So he did.

Of course, Simba had to get used to a few things, such as having no zebras or antelopes or hippos to eat. Instead, Timon introduced him to a new kind of food, grubs! The cub also ate termites, ladybugs and all the other insects that crawled around the jungle.

"You'll learn to love them!" Pumbaa told him.

Simba didn't think he ever would, but he ate them anyway.

What the lion cub *did* love were his new friends.

With Timon and Pumbaa, every day brought new games and fun-filled adventures. When they weren't playing, they were eating; when they weren't eating, they were playing; and when they weren't doing either, they just relaxed.

As the years went by, the friends grew closer and closer and Simba's sad past faded away . . . almost.

One day, while Timon and Pumbaa were out stalking beetles, a stranger appeared in the jungle, a fierce lioness, alone and very hungry!

"*Aaaaggh!*" yelled Pumbaa, as he fled. The warthog got stuck beneath an old tree root as he tried to run away.

"*Aaaaggh!*" screamed Timon, as he tried to push Pumbaa to freedom before the lioness attacked them.

Luckily, Simba heard his friends' cries and raced to their defense. Now fully grown, he easily wrestled the lioness to the ground, but she quickly flipped him over and pinned *him* down. Only then did he realize whom he was fighting.

"Nala?" he said. She was one of his old playmates!

Nala was surprised to see him. Scar had told the whole pride that Simba was dead! She told her old friend that Scar had let the hyenas take over the Pride Lands. "Everything's destroyed. There's no food or water. You're our only hope!" she cried.

When Timon, Pumbaa and Nala woke up the next morning, Simba was gone.

"The king has returned," Rafiki informed them.

At first, Timon and Pumbaa didn't understand. But Nala did. She told them about Scar and how he had taken over as king and ruined the once great Pride Lands.

"Simba must fight his uncle to take his place as king," she explained. She also told them that he might need a little help.

"If it's important to Simba," Timon said, "we're with him to the end."

Timon, Pumbaa and Nala hurried to catch up with Simba. They followed him to the Pride Lands.

Once there, Simba let out an earthshaking roar and climbed Pride Rock to face his evil uncle.

"Step down, Scar," Simba commanded.

But his uncle wasn't going to give up the kingdom so easily. Scar and the hyenas fought and soon Simba was dangling from a cliff.

"This is just the way your father looked before he died," sneered Scar.

Suddenly, Simba realized that Scar was the one responsible for Mufasa's death - not him! Filled with rage, he sprang onto the ledge. With Timon, Pumbaa and Nala beside him, he took on Scar and the hyenas.

The friends fought bravely. Scar attacked Simba, but the younger lion quickly moved out of the way. Scar fell to his death. The hyenas soon retreated. The battle over, Simba immediately became king.

Under Simba's wise and just rule,
the Pride Lands soon returned to their
former splendour. Simba went on to
become as great a king as his father.
He and Nala soon had a cub of
their own.

The Circle of Life continued,
as it was always meant to. Simba
lived happily ever after . . . along with
two better and truer friends than
any lion king ever had!

WALT DISNEY'S

Lady and the TRAMP

Unlikely Friends

Lady, a beautiful Cocker Spaniel, loved her owners. The day that she first came home, she overheard them talking to each other and realized their names must be Jim Dear and Darling. Every morning, Lady woke Jim Dear for work. She brought him his slippers and fetched the newspaper. During the day Lady kept Darling company and they always enjoyed an afternoon walk together.

When Lady was six months old, she received her first collar and license. After Darling put it on her, Lady happily pranced outside. She was excited to show her best friends, Jock the Scottish terrier and Trusty the bloodhound.

They both admired her license and Lady held her head high. She was so proud!

On the other side of town, Tramp was a mutt who wasn't what most people would have called respectable. He didn't have owners or a home of his own. He was footloose and collar-free, but he was also very clever. He had a good heart and often rescued his friends from the clutches of the dogcatcher. He didn't want them to have to go to the pound.

Tramp loved going on chases. One afternoon, he tricked and teased the dogcatcher until he'd lost him. Then he looked around and noticed he was in a very smart part of town.

"Snob Hill," he muttered. He was glad he didn't live in this kind of neighbourhood. It looked boring. "Wonder what the leash-and-collar set does for excitement."

Curious, Tramp wandered into a yard and overheard Lady and her friends. "It's something I've done, I guess," Lady was saying sadly. "Jim Dear and Darling are acting so strangely."

Jock and Trusty simply smiled. They knew what the problem was. Darling was expecting a baby!

Lady was confused. "What's a baby?" she asked.

"Just a cute little bundle of trouble," Tramp piped up.

Lady looked bewildered. She'd never seen this strange dog before. He didn't even have a collar on!

Tramp continued. "Remember those nice juicy cuts of beef? Forget 'em. Leave that nice warm bed by the fire? How about a leaky doghouse instead?"

Jock told Lady not to listen to the dog. Then turned to Tramp and told him to leave.

"Okay, okay," Tramp replied. Before he left, he warned Lady, "Remember, when a baby moves in, the dog moves out!"

Lady was worried, but luckily Tramp's predictions did not come true. When the baby was born, Darling showed her to Lady, who loved the child instantly!

Every day, Lady watched over the baby. Jim Dear and Darling petted her proudly. When they decided to take a short holiday, they knew the baby would be in good hands. Besides, Darling's aunt, Sarah, would be there to help.

Aunt Sarah however, would not let Lady near the baby. Even worse, she had brought two sneaky Siamese cats with her. When Aunt Sarah was out of the room, the cats tried to eat the goldfish. Then they ripped the curtains. Lady tried to stop the cats, but her barking angered Aunt Sarah.

"Oh! Merciful heavens!" Aunt Sarah cried when she came downstairs. The cats had made it look like Lady had messed up the room and attacked *them*.

Aunt Sarah was furious. She dragged Lady to the pet store to fit her with a muzzle! Lady was upset as she hadn't done anything wrong. As soon as the salesman put the muzzle on her, Lady ran out of the store. Cars screeched by. Tin cans got caught on her leash and made a horrendous racket. When ferocious dogs started chasing her, Lady was terrified.

Suddenly, Tramp appeared! He fought the bullies and rescued Lady.

"What are you doing on this side of the tracks?" he asked.

Just then he noticed the muzzle. "Aw, you poor kid. We've got to get this thing off. Come on!" he said.

Tramp led Lady through town to the zoo. There, they found a beaver building a dam. The beaver easily bit through the muzzle strap and freed Lady!

Lady felt grateful; both to the beaver and to Tramp.

Tramp wanted to show Lady how great life could be for a dog who wasn't part of a family. He decided to take her to a special Italian restaurant. Tony, the owner, loved Tramp.

"Where you been-a so long?" Tony asked. "What's this-a? Hey, Joe, look; he's gotta new girlfriend."

Lady blushed.

"Tonight-a he's getting best in the house!" Tony said to Joe, who worked at the restaurant.

"Okay, Tony," said Joe. "You're da boss."

Tramp and Lady looked at the menu. Then Tramp barked.

Tony knew exactly what Tramp wanted and before long, he returned with a huge platter of spaghetti and meatballs. Then he and Joe serenaded the dogs.

Without meaning to, the dogs began to eat the same piece of spaghetti. They didn't realize what had happened until their lips met in a kiss. Then Tramp rolled the last meatball towards Lady.

She was touched by his generosity. Tramp was different from what she had thought. He felt the same way about her. As they stared into each other's eyes, it was clear that they had fallen in love.

It was a beautiful night. Lady and Tramp walked side by side through empty streets. The sky was lit with stars and the moon was full. They went to a grassy hill in the park and fell asleep.

The next morning Lady was worried. "I should have been home hours ago!" she cried. Unlike Tramp, she liked belonging to a family.

Tramp wanted to chase chickens to show Lady how much fun his life was. Unfortunately, a dogcatcher appeared and threw Lady in his wagon.

When Aunt Sarah picked Lady up from the pound, she was so angry that she chained her to the doghouse.

Lady was heartbroken. Now she wouldn't be able to see the baby.

That evening, Lady saw a rat climb through the window of the baby's room! She barked wildly, trying to warn Aunt Sarah.

The old woman simply opened the window and yelled at her. "Hush now! Stop that racket!"

Luckily, Tramp was nearby and heard Lady's cries. "What's wrong?" he asked.

"A rat! Upstairs in the baby's room!" Lady cried.

Bravely, Tramp raced into the house through the doggie door. Lady finally broke free from her chain and followed him up to the baby's room. Tramp fought the rat; and won! Although the two knocked over everything in sight, the baby was safe. Lady was so proud of Tramp.

Aunt Sarah came into the room but did not see the rat. She only saw that the crib had been knocked over.

She locked Lady in the cellar and shoved Tramp into a closet. Then she called to have the dogcatcher take Tramp away.

Jim Dear and Darling arrived home just as the dogcatcher
was putting Tramp in his wagon.

"What's going on here?" asked Jim Dear.

"Just picking up a stray, mister," said the dogcatcher. "Caught
him attacking a baby."

Jim Dear and Darling looked at each other worriedly and
rushed inside. "Aunt Sarah? Aunt Sarah!" they called.

The old woman tried to explain what had happened. Against
her wishes, Jim Dear and Darling let Lady out of the cellar. The
Cocker Spaniel quickly ran upstairs, barking.

"Keep her away!" Aunt Sarah cried.

"Nonsense," said Jim Dear. "She's trying to tell us something.
What is it, old girl?"

Lady led him to the baby's room and uncovered the dead rat.
Jim Dear realized what had happened. Tramp was a hero! Jim
Dear and Lady went to rescue him.

Jim Dear and Lady brought Tramp home and he became part of their family. Soon he had his very own license. But he didn't mind one bit, as it meant that he could always be with Lady.

By Christmas, Lady and Tramp had four puppies of their own. With wonderful friends and a loving family, Lady and Tramp lived happily ever after.

Love Conquers All

One day, long ago, a beautiful fox named Maid Marian was playing badminton in the courtyard of Nottingham Castle with her lady-in-waiting, Lady Kluck. Nearby, a young rabbit named Skippy was practising his archery. When one of the arrows flew into the courtyard, he went to retrieve it and bumped into Maid Marian.

His friends soon followed him. They hadn't seen Maid Marian up close before. "Gee, you're very beautiful," a small bunny named Tagalong said to her.

"Are you gonna marry Robin Hood?" another rabbit asked.

"Mama says you and Robin Hood are sweethearts," Tagalong piped up.

"That was several years ago, before I left for London," Maid Marian replied. Then she showed the children the tree in which Robin Hood had carved their initials. "He's probably forgotten all about me," she remarked.

Later, after the children had left, Maid Marian sat in the castle, thinking about Robin Hood. He was a dashing fox and they had been in love. King Richard, a brave lion and Maid Marian's uncle, had left to fight a battle and she had not seen Robin Hood since then. In King Richard's absence, his brother, Prince John, who was also a lion, had seized power.

The prince was very greedy and tried to get his hands on all of the money he could. He even stole from the poorest members of his kingdom. Robin Hood would not stand for it. He stole money from the rich and gave it back to the poor. Prince John hated him and declared him an outlaw.

Marian glanced at the WANTED poster of Robin Hood that she kept in her room. She wondered if he knew how much she loved him?

Meanwhile, in Sherwood Forest, Robin Hood and his bear friend, Little John, were doing chores in their hideout. Little John hung up clothing and Robin Hood cooked dinner. But it wasn't long before the pot boiled over. The fox was distracted.

"You're burning the chow!" Little John cried.

"Sorry," Robin replied. "I guess I was thinking about Maid Marian again."

"Why don't you stop moonin' and mopin' around? Just marry the girl," Little John said.

"Marry her?" Robin replied. "What have I got to offer her? She's a highborn lady of quality. I'm an outlaw." He couldn't stop daydreaming about her though, he was in love.

A while later, a badger named Friar Tuck arrived. He told Robin and Little John about an archery tournament that the prince was holding the next day. Robin knew he could win the contest, but he didn't want to risk getting arrested.

Friar Tuck then told him what the prize was: a kiss from Maid Marian. Robin Hood made a decision instantly. He would go to the tournament and win it; along with Maid Marian's heart. Somehow, he would do it without getting arrested.

The next day, Robin Hood and Little John disguised themselves and went to the tournament. Robin Hood was dressed as a stork and Little John wore a duke's costume. He walked right up to the Sheriff of Nottingham and said "hello". When the Sheriff didn't recognize him, Robin Hood knew his plan would work!

Meanwhile, Maid Marian and Lady Kluck had arrived at
the tournament. The beautiful fox had a feeling that she would
see Robin Hood.

"Oh, Klucky, I'm so excited," Maid Marian said. "But how
will I recognize him?"

"Oh, he'll let you know somehow," Lady Kluck replied.
"That young rogue of yours is
full of surprises."

They made their way
over to the royal box,
where Maid Marian
would be watching the
tournament.

Marian sat on one side of Prince John in the royal box. On the prince's other side was Little John. He'd done such an amazing job of disguising himself that the prince thought he was the Duke of Chutney!

Soon, the archers paraded by the royal box. No one knew Robin Hood was one of them, not even Maid Marian. The outlaw went up to her and handed her a flower.

"It's a great honour to be shootin' for the favour of a lovely lady like yourself," Robin told her. Then he winked at her. "I hope I win the kiss."

Maid Marian realized who the stork really was. "I wish you luck," she said, "with all my heart."

The archers began to shoot. Robin Hood hit one bull's-eye after another. A few rounds later, only two contestants were left: the Sheriff and Robin Hood. The target was moved back an extra thirty paces. The Sheriff hit the target. Then, as Robin was taking aim, the Sheriff knocked into him with his bow to try to sabotage the contest.

The arrow traveled upward, but quick as a wink, Robin shot another arrow at the first one, which sent it down towards the target and straight into the bull's-eye.

It was so accurate that it even split the Sheriff's arrow in two!

Robin Hood had won the contest!

However, Robin Hood went to collect his kiss from Maid Marian, the prince realized who he was. He used his sword to cut the fox's disguise away.

"Seize him!" Prince John ordered his men. "I sentence you to instant and even immediate, death."

Maid Marian began to sob. "Please, sire. I beg of you to spare his life."

"Why should I?" the prince replied coldly.

"Because I love him, Your Highness," she replied.

Marian loves me! the fox thought. I have won her heart!

"My darling, I love you more than life itself," Robin Hood declared.

The beautiful fox was elated. Now she knew how he really felt.

But Prince John didn't care. He decided Robin Hood should die.

Luckily, Little John was standing nearby. He held a dagger to the prince's back, convincing the ruler to free Robin Hood.

Then a fight broke out. The guards fought Robin Hood and Little John. Even Lady Kluck took part. She flipped the Sheriff over her head and onto the ground.

But Maid Marian got caught in the middle of all the fighting. Suddenly, guards were running towards her. "Help!" she called.

Robin Hood leaped up and grabbed onto a rope, swinging across the field to rescue his lady love. He swooped her up and they swung towards the royal box, where he asked Marian for her hand in marriage. She accepted as he fought more guards.

Finally, they were able to escape, along with Little John and Lady Kluck. They all went back to Sherwood Forest, where they met Friar Tuck and the rest of Robin's band of merry men and celebrated with some dancing.

Prince John was very angry that Robin Hood had escaped. He decided to collect more taxes from everyone. When Friar Tuck wouldn't pay, he was thrown in jail. The prince sentenced him to death to lure Robin Hood back.

But the outlaw couldn't be caught that easily. He snuck into the prison and released the Friar and all the other poor folk. Then, he stole the prince's gold and gave it to the poor.

Eventually, King Richard came back and took over.

Because he was a just and fair king, everything in the kingdom went back to the way it had been and Robin Hood no longer had to steal.

The king pardoned Robin Hood, which meant that he and Maid Marian could finally get married! All of their friends went to the ceremony. They had a wonderful celebration.

Marian and Robin couldn't have been happier. At long last, they were together, forever.

DISNEY'S THE LITTLE MERMAID

Sebastian Helps Out

Beneath the sea, all of the merfolk gathered at King Triton's royal palace for a concert. Sebastian the crab, the court composer, was excited for everyone to hear his new symphony. He gestured for the orchestra to begin playing.

Everything went very smoothly until a large seashell opened. Ariel, the king's youngest daughter, was supposed to emerge from the shell and begin to sing. She had a lovely voice and it was always a treat to hear her. However, when the shell opened, it was empty!

King Triton couldn't believe that his daughter hadn't shown up.

Sebastian couldn't believe it, either. The concert was ruined!

Ariel was busy exploring a sunken ship with her friend Flounder. She had completely forgotten about the concert. She finally remembered and swam straight home.

King Triton was furious when he found out where she had been. He believed that humans were dangerous. "I am never, never to hear of you going to the surface again!" he warned.

Ariel swam off. King Triton turned to Sebastian. "Ariel needs constant supervision," he said. "And you are just the crab to do it."

Sebastian was speechless. He didn't want to look after Ariel, but he couldn't refuse the king. He sank down in his shell, muttering to himself. "How do I get myself in these situations? I should be writing symphonies, not tagging along after some headstrong teenager."

That day, Sebastian began keeping an eye on Ariel. He followed her and Flounder to her secret grotto. It was filled from floor to ceiling with human objects that she had collected from sunken ships. He hid and listened quietly as the young mermaid sang about her dream to be part of the human world. He was so shocked that he lost his footing and fell off a ledge.

Ariel realized that he had been following her. "What is all this?" Sebastian exclaimed. "If your father knew about this place . . ."

The mermaid begged Sebastian not to tell King Triton. At that moment, a ship sailing overhead caught her attention and she began to swim towards it.

"Ariel?" the crab called. Then he realized she was swimming towards the surface. "Jumping jellyfish!" he shouted. "Come back!"

By the time Sebastian and Flounder reached the surface, a hurricane had begun and the ship was sinking.

Ariel had rescued a human and was pulling him to shore. The human's name was Prince Eric and the mermaid thought he was very handsome. He was everything she had ever dreamed about!

Because the prince was unconscious, Ariel stayed by his side, even singing to him. Ariel heard his servant coming, she dove into the water. She didn't want anyone to know she was a mermaid. She watched with Sebastian and Flounder as the prince awakened and returned to the palace with his servant.

Sebastian knew that King Triton would be very angry if he found out what Ariel had done. "We're just going to forget this whole thing ever happened," he told Ariel and Flounder.

129

But Ariel couldn't stop thinking about Prince Eric.

Sebastian tried to reason with her. "Will you get your head out of the clouds and back in the water where it belongs?"

More than ever, Ariel wanted to be among humans. The crab couldn't convince her that life under the sea was better than life in the surface world. Then, by accident, he revealed to the king that Ariel was in love with a human.

King Triton was furious. He went to see his daughter at once.

"Have you completely lost your senses?" he bellowed. "He's a human. You're a mermaid!"

"I don't care," Ariel said defiantly.

The king raised his trident and destroyed all of Ariel's human objects. After he left, Sebastian tried to apologize.

"Just go away," the mermaid said, sobbing.

Sebastian felt awful.

Ariel's crying was cut short by the arrival of two wicked eels who worked for Ursula, the sea witch. They led the mermaid to their boss's cave. Sebastian and Flounder followed them.

Ursula offered Ariel a deal: she would give her human legs in exchange for her voice. "I will make you a potion that will turn you into a human for three days," the sea witch said. "If the prince kisses you before the sun sets on the third day, you'll remain human permanently. If he doesn't, you'll turn back into a mermaid and you'll belong to me!"

Ariel knew it was her only chance to get to know Prince Eric. Reluctantly, she signed her name on the contract. Moments later, Ursula had captured the mermaid's voice in a shell and transformed her tail into two human legs! Sebastian and Flounder rushed over to help Ariel. Now that she was human, she couldn't stay underwater for very long.

When Ariel made it to the rocky shore, she was greeted by another one of her friends, Scuttle the seagull.

Sebastian was beside himself. "This is a catastrophe! What would her father say? I'm going to march myself straight home right now and tell him!"

Ariel shook her head at him, since she had no voice.

"Don't you shake your head at me, young lady!" said Sebastian. Then he smiled hopefully. "Maybe there's still time. If we could get that witch to give you back your voice, you could go home

with all the normal fish and just be . . . just be . . ."

The little mermaid looked at him pleadingly.

Sebastian sighed. "Just be miserable for the rest of your life," he finished. He knew he couldn't turn his back on his friend. "All right. I'll try to help you find that prince."

Ariel was so thrilled and relieved, she gave the crab a kiss.

"Boy, what a soft shell I'm turning out to be," Sebastian said.

Scuttle located some rope and sailcloth with which to make a dress for Ariel.

Before long, Prince Eric found Ariel. Although she couldn't speak, Eric was still enchanted by her. One afternoon, he took her for a boat ride in a lush lagoon. Sebastian helped create a romantic mood by getting the lagoon's creatures to sing and play music.

Just as the prince was about to kiss Ariel, their rowboat tipped over! Ursula had sent her two eels to make sure Eric and Ariel didn't kiss.

Through a magical glass ball, Ursula watched Ariel and Eric topple out of the boat. "Nice work, boys," she said to the eels. "That was a close one."

But Ursula was still worried that the prince might kiss Ariel before sunset the next day, so she formulated a wicked plan. She plotted to turn herself into a pretty young woman named Vanessa. She would then use Ariel's voice, which was locked inside the shell on a cord around her neck, to sound like the little mermaid and win the prince's heart.

That evening, Vanessa went ashore and sang to Prince Eric. He was captivated; she sounded just like the girl who had rescued him. When Vanessa put a spell on him, the prince insisted that they be married the very next day.

Ariel was heartbroken when she heard the news, but there was nothing she could do. She had no idea that Vanessa was really Ursula in disguise.

The next day, Ariel, Flounder and Sebastian were sitting at the dock when Scuttle flew up. He explained that he had seen Vanessa looking in a mirror and her reflection had revealed that she was really Ursula!

Ariel and her friends knew they had to stop the wedding. Sebastian cut a barrel loose and said to Flounder, "Get her to that boat as fast as your fins can carry you! I've got to get to the sea king!" He told Scuttle to stall the wedding.

Ariel hung onto the barrel as Flounder pulled it towards the ship. When she got there, Scuttle yanked the shell from Vanessa's neck. Ariel got her voice back and the spell on Eric was broken. Before they could kiss, the sun set and Ariel turned back into a mermaid. Vanessa transformed into Ursula and dragged the mermaid underwater. Prince Eric didn't want to lose Ariel, so he fought the sea witch in a fierce battle and won.

Although Ursula had been defeated, Ariel was still a mermaid. She couldn't live in Prince Eric's world.

King Triton saw how unhappy his daughter was. "She really does love him, doesn't she?" he said to Sebastian.

The crab nodded.

"Then I guess there's just one problem left," said King Triton.

"What's that, Your Majesty?" asked Sebastian.

"How much I'm going to miss her," King Triton explained. Then, with a flash of golden light from his trident, he gave Ariel human legs.

Sebastian was truly happy for Ariel. He would miss her, too, but he was sure that they would see each other again soon.

Walt Disney's Bambi

The Winter Trail

One winter morning, Bambi the young deer was dozing in the wood when he heard a thumping sound nearby.

"C'mon, Bambi!" his bunny friend, Thumper, cried. "It's a perfect day for playing."

Bambi slowly got up and followed Thumper through the forest. It was a beautiful day! The sky was blue and sunny and the ground was covered in a blanket of new snow. Icicles glistened on the trees.

"Look at these tracks!" Thumper said excitedly. He pointed to a line of footprints in the snow. "I saw them on the way over. Who do you suppose they belong to?"

Bambi didn't know so they decided to follow the trail. They pranced and hopped through the snow. Before long, they came to the tree and saw someone who might have left the tracks.

"Wake up, Friend Owl!" called Thumper.

The bird peered down at the animals. He had only just flown to his favourite tree branch and fallen asleep. "Stop that racket!" he replied crossly and closed his eyes.

Bambi and Thumper giggled. Friend Owl was always grouchy when they woke him up.

"Friend Owl, have you been out walking?" Bambi asked.

"Now why would I do that?" Friend Owl replied, opening his eyes. "My wings take me everywhere I need to go."

Bambi and Thumper continued on.

Soon, they met up with Bambi's friend Faline. "You can help us find out who made these tracks," said Bambi, pointing to the trail.

Thumper thumped his foot impatiently. He wanted to keep going.

Faline nodded and began to walk with them.

Thumper hopped ahead quickly. Maybe their friend Flower the skunk wanted to come, too.

But Flower was hibernating. Thumper's mother had told him that meant the skunk would be sleeping all winter long.

When Thumper tried to wake Flower, the little skunk just mumbled, "See you next spring," without even opening his eyes.

The three friends decided to keep going without him.

Thumper bounded ahead. He followed the footprints to a frozen pond and glided across. "Come on!" he called. "There are tracks over here, too."

So, Faline and Bambi started to cross the pond. Before long, Faline had joined Thumper on the other side. Unlike his friends, Bambi was not a very good skater. His legs went out from under him and he fell on the ice.

"Aw, Bambi, come on," Thumper urged. "We can go skating later. I'll even show you how to spin around."

After a lot of slipping and sliding, Bambi finally took a running start and sped across the pond on his belly.

Next, the three friends walked up a snowy hill. At the top, they spotted a raccoon sitting next to a tree trunk, eating some red berries.

"Hello, Mr Raccoon," Faline said. "Did you happen to see who made these tracks in the snow?"

The raccoon's mouth was so full he couldn't say anything. He shook his head and began tapping the tree.

The friends looked around. Then they heard a "tap, tap, tap" in the distance.

"I know!" Thumper cried. "He thinks we should ask the woodpeckers."

"Oh, thank you," Bambi said. The raccoon waved good-bye as the friends headed towards a row of pine trees.

The tapping got louder and louder. Soon, Bambi, Faline and Thumper had found the woodpeckers. The mother was pecking away and her three children were sitting in holes in the tree trunk. They stuck their heads out when they heard Thumper cry, "Helloooooo!"

The mother bird stopped her pecking. "Yes?" she asked.

"Well, you see," Bambi began shyly, "we were wondering . . . that is, we're looking for - "

"Aw, for Pete's sake," Thumper interrupted. "Did you make the tracks in the snow?" he called up to the birds.

"No, we've been here all day," the mother bird answered.

"Yes, yes, yes," her babies added.

Just then, Faline noticed that the trail continued. "Thank you," she called to the birds.

She rushed ahead, while Bambi and Thumper walked slowly. "If the tracks don't belong to the woodpeckers and they don't belong to the raccoon and they don't belong to Friend Owl, whose can they be?" Bambi asked his rabbit friend.

"I don't know," Thumper replied, frustrated.

They soon reached the end of the trail. The tracks led all the way to a snowy bush, where a family of quail were resting. "Hello!" Mrs Quail cooed as the deer and rabbit approached.

"Did you make these tracks?" Thumper asked her.

"Why, yes," Mrs Quail answered. "Friend Owl told me about this wonderful bush. So this morning, my babies and I walked all the way over here."

Thumper and Bambi nodded. Then Thumper pointed to the edge of the glen. Faline was there. "Mrs Quail invited us to join her for a snack, so I was just getting some leaves," she said. The three friends sat down to eat with the quail family.

The sun was getting low in the sky and it was time for the friends to go home. They'd spent all day following the trail! When they turned to leave, a big surprise was waiting for them; their mothers!

Bambi bounded over to his mother and stretched his nose up for a kiss. "We've been looking for you," she told him tenderly.

Thumper was surprised. "How'd ya find us?" he asked.

Thumper's mother said, "Well, your sisters pointed us in the right direction and then. . ." She looked down at the deer and rabbit tracks that the three friends had left in the snow.

"You followed our trail!" Faline cried. Her mother nodded.

"Now, let's follow it back home," Bambi's mother said.

So that's just what they did.